Salamatu
go missing

By Steve Brace

Illustrated by Annie Kubler

Published by Child's Play (Internatio

Swindon   Auburn ME

© 2000 Child's Play®   ISBN 0-85953-784-6   Printed in India

A catalogue reference for this book is available from the British Library.

Salamatu lives with her brothers and sisters
in a village called Nansoni in Ghana.

Ghana is a country in Africa.

Salamatu has a goat
called Kandoni.

Goats provide milk
for the village.

Kandoni has a black mark
on her right ear.

Every morning,
Salamatu feeds Kandoni.

One morning, Kandoni
follows Salamatu
on her way to school.

"Go back home!"
Salamatu cries

Kandoni takes no notice.

**"If I pick you
a nice juicy mango,
will you go home?"**

Salamatu's mother has told her
not to climb trees.
But how else can she pick
a mango for Kandoni?

Besides, Salamatu likes climbing trees.

Salamatu likes mangoes, too!

She is so busy eating mangoes
that she forgets about Kandoni.

When Salamatu climbs
down the tree,
Kandoni is nowhere
to be seen.

"I am in real trouble now.
I have lost Kandoni.
If only I had not
climbed up the tree."

Salamatu looks everywhere.

**"I am looking for Kandoni.
Have you seen her?
I am going to be
late for school."**

Some women are carrying
firewood to the village.

"Have you seen
my goat?"

"No, dear.
Ask at the tree
nursery."

In the tree nursery,
young trees are being watered.

"Have you seen my goat?
She has a black mark
on her right ear."

"Sorry, we have not seen her.
Ask Ibrahima. He is over there
in the yam field."

No luck.

Hasmiyd and Admidu
are fetching water from the dam.

"Salamatu, why are you
not in school?
It is a quarter to ten."

"Oh, no!
It is too late for school now.
And I still have to find Kandoni!"

In the village square,
Salamatu's father is praying at the mosque.

"I hope he has not seen me," she thinks.

There is no sign of Kandoni.

At the school, Salamatu
whispers to her friend.

**"Ssh!
Have you seen
my goat?"**

In the market place, everyone
is too busy to look for the goat.

Suddenly, Salamatu
hears bleating.

MEH!
MEH!

Not one goat, but twenty-five!

"Let us check them, anyway," says Kojo.
"You never know!"

Surely, somebody
must have seen
Salamatu's goat?

The children are already
out of school.

"Please, help me find Kandoni,"
Salamatu asks her friends.

But everybody seems so busy!

"Mother! Father!
Where is Salamatu?
She was not at school."

Salamatu's parents set off
to look for her.

"I will go
this way."

"Salamatu!
Where have you been?"

"I am sorry, Mother.
I did not mean to miss school."

"I have been looking
or Kandoni.

She followed me
and I climbed
up a tree to fetch
her a mango.

When I climbed down,
she had gone."

Salamatu frowns.
Why are her mother
and father laughing?

Then she feels
something tickling
her heel.

"Kandoni, there you are!
I am so happy to see you!

But, promise me
you will never
make me miss
school again!"

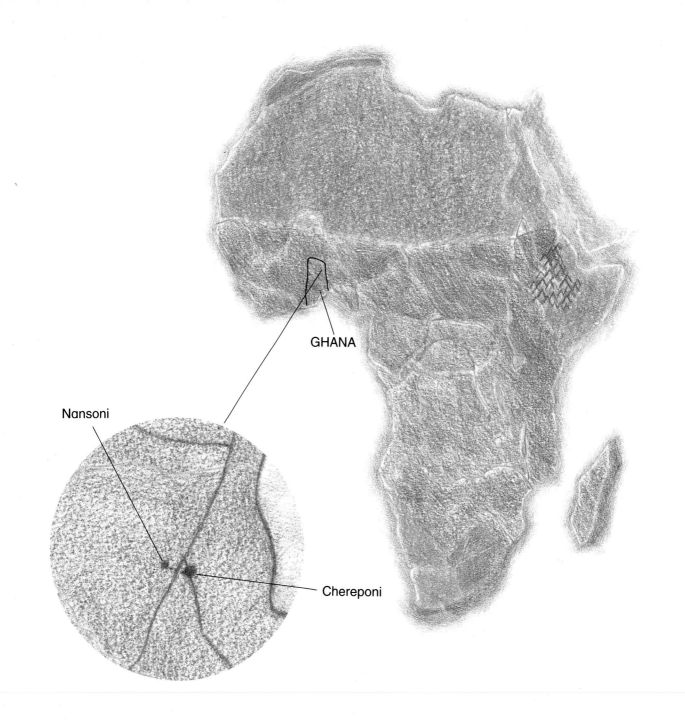

GHANA

Nansoni

Chereponi